Charles F. Bahnson

North Carolina Lodge Manual

For the Degrees of Entered Apprentice, Fellow Craft, and Master Mason,

as Authorized by the Grand Lodge of North Carolina Free and Accepted

Masons: and the Services for the Burial of the Dead of the Fraternity

Charles F. Bahnson

North Carolina Lodge Manual
For the Degrees of Entered Apprentice, Fellow Craft, and Master Mason, as Authorized by the Grand Lodge of North Carolina Free and Accepted Masons: and the Services for the Burial of the Dead of the Fraternity

ISBN/EAN: 9783337394929

Printed in Europe, USA, Canada, Australia, Japan

Cover: Foto ©Andreas Hilbeck / pixelio.de

More available books at **www.hansebooks.com**

NORTH CAROLINA

LODGE MANUAL

FOR THE DEGREES OF

ENTERED APPRENTICE, FELLOW CRAFT AND MASTER MASON,

AS AUTHORIZED BY THE

GRAND LODGE OF NORTH CAROLINA,
ANCIENT FREE AND ACCEPTED MASONS,

AND THE

SERVICES FOR THE BURIAL OF THE DEAD OF THE FRATERNITY.

BY

CHARLES F. BAHNSON, P. M.,
ASSISTANT GRAND LECTURER.

FARMINGTON, N. C.
1892.

TO

SAMUEL H. SMITH,

P. G. M. OF THE GRAND LODGE OF NORTH CAROLINA.

M. W. SIR AND BRO.:

Esteeming you as a comrade in time of war, and a friend and brother in time of peace, and knowing your zealous and ardent attachment to the principles of Masonry, I desire in token of my respect to dedicate this work to you.

CHARLES F. BAHNSON.

FARMINGTON, N. C., 1892.

"The following was presented by Bro. Chas. F. Bahnson, and the permission asked was granted:

"To the Most Worshipful Grand Lodge of North Carolina:

"As there is a great need of a Manual adapted to the work of this Grand Jurisdiction, I respectfully ask permission to publish one, after being examined by the Grand Lecturer, and approved by the Most Worshipful Grand Master.

"Respectfully,

"CHAS. F. BAHNSON,

"*Asst. Grand Lecturer.*"

"M. W. H. A. GUDGER,

Grand Master of Masons, Asheville, N. C.:

"*Dear Sir and Bro.:*—I have carefully examined the manuscript of the proposed 'North Carolina Lodge Manual,' compiled by Bro. Chas. F. Bahnson, Asst. Grand Lecturer, and have no hesitancy in giving it my unqualified endorsement, and commend it to the favorable consideration of the Craft for cheapness, conciseness, and convenience.

"Fraternally yours,

"B. W. HATCHER,

"*Grand Lecturer A. F. & A. M. for the State at Large, and Custodian of the Work.*"

(4)

"CHAS. F. BAHNSON, *Asst. Grand Lecturer :*

" *Dear Sir and Bro.:*—In obedience to the resolution of the Grand Lodge, I have given the manuscript for your Masonic Manual a careful examination, and do not hesitate to give it my most hearty endorsement and approval.

"I take great pleasure in recommending it to those who are in search of Masonic light.

" Yours fraternally,

" H. A. GUDGER,

" *Grand Master.*"

CONTENTS.

MANUAL OF THE LODGE.

PRAYERS AND ODES.

OPENING.

Music—"*Old Hundred.*"—L. M.

Great God, oehold before thy throne,
  A band of brothers lowly bend;
Thy sacred Name we humbly own,
  And pray that thou wilt be our friend.

A band of brothers may we live,
  A band of brothers may we die,
To each may God, our Father, give
  A home of peace above the sky.

PRAYER.

Most holy and glorious Lord God, the great
Architect of the Universe, the giver of all good
gifts and graces : Thou hast promised that
" where two or three are gathered together in
thy name, thou wilt be in the midst of them, and
bless them." In thy name we assemble, most
humbly beseeching thee to bless us in all our undertakings, that we may know and serve thee
aright, and that all our actions may tend to thy
glory, and to our advancement in knowledge and

(7)

virtue. And we beseech thee, O Lord God, to bless our present assembling, and to illuminate our minds, that we may walk in the light of thy countenance; and when the trials of our probationary state are over, be admitted into "The Temple," not made with hands, eternal in the heavens.

Response by the brethren—So mote it be. Amen.

CLOSING.

MUSIC—"*Nearer, my God, to Thee.*"

> Brothers, we meet again,
>   Too soon to part;
> May Friendship bless this hour,
>   And warm each heart;
> Tones that we love to hear,
> Shall dwell upon the ear,
> As we in accents clear,
>   Repeat Good-night.

> Brothers, once more farewell!
>   Time bids us part;
> Fond mem'ry long shall dwell
>   Around each heart;
> May Heav'n its blessings send
> And peace our paths attend;
> Until we meet again,
>   Farewell, Good-night.

PRAYER.

Supreme Architect of the Universe, accept our humble praises for the many mercies and blessings which thy bounty has conferred on us, and especially for this friendly and social intercourse. Pardon, we beseech thee, whatever thou hast seen amiss in us since we have been together; and continue to us thy presence, protection, and blessing. Make us sensible of the renewed obligations we are under to love thee supremely, and to be friendly to each other. May all our irregular passions be subdued, and may we daily increase in *Faith, Hope,* and *Charity;* but more especially in that charity which is the bond of peace and perfection of every virtue. May we so practice thy precepts, that we may finally obtain thy promises, and find an entrance through the gates into the temple and city of our God.

Response—So mote it be. Amen.

* * * * * * *

Level. Plumb. Square.

* * * * * * *

BENEDICTION.

May the blessing of Heaven rest upon us and all regular Masons! May brotherly love prevail, and every moral and social virtue cement us.

Response—So mote it be. Amen.

CHARGE AT CLOSING.

BRETHREN:—We are now about to quit this sacred retreat of friendship and virtue, to mix again with the world. Amidst its concerns and employments, forget not the duties which you have heard so frequently inculcated, and so forcibly recommended, in this Lodge. Be diligent, prudent, temperate, discreet. Remember that, around this altar, you have promised to befriend and relieve every brother who shall need your assistance. You have promised, in the most friendly manner, to remind him of his errors, and aid a reformation. These generous principles are to extend further. Every human being has a claim upon your kind offices. Do good unto all. Recommend it more especially "to the household of the faithful." Finally, brethren, be ye all of one mind; live in peace; and may the God of love and peace delight to dwell with and bless you.

"Freemasonry, a beautiful system of morality, veiled in allegory, and illustrated by symbols." The most ancient society in the world; its principles are based on pure morality, its ethics are the ethics of pure religion; its doctrines, the doctrines of brotherly love; and its sentiments, the sentiments of exalted benevolence. It encourages all that is good, kind, and charitable; and reproves all that is vicious, cruel, and oppressive.

ENTERED APPRENTICE'S DEGREE.

PRELIMINARIES TO THE ADMISSION OF CANDIDATES.

Before a candidate shall be prepared for initiation, he shall answer satisfactorily the following interrogatories:

1. Do you declare upon your honor, before these witnesses, that unbiased by friends, and uninfluenced by mercenary motives, you freely and voluntarily offer yourself a candidate for the mysteries of Masonry?

2. Do you further declare upon your honor, before these witnesses, that you are prompted to solicit the privileges of Masonry, by a favorable opinion conceived of the Institution, a desire of knowledge, and a sincere wish to be serviceable to your fellow-creatures?

3. Do you further declare upon your honor, before these witnesses, that you will cheerfully conform to all the ancient established usages and customs of the Fraternity?

4. Have you petitioned any other Lodge and been rejected by it?

(11)

FIRST SECTION.

ADMISSION OF THE CANDIDATE.

PRAYER.

Vouchsafe thine aid, Almighty Father of the Universe, to this our present convention; and grant that this candidate for Masonry may dedicate and devote his life to thy service, and become a true and faithful brother among us! Endue him with a competency of thy divine wisdom, that by the secrets of our art he may be better enabled to display the beauties of holiness, to the honor of thy holy name. So mote it be. Amen.

*   *   *   *   *   *   *

"Behold, how good and how pleasant it is for brethren to dwell together in unity!

"It is like the precious ointment upon the head, that ran down upon the beard, even Aaron's beard; that went down to the skirts of his garments:

"As the dew of Hermon, and as the dew that descended upon the mountains of Zion : for there the Lord commanded the blessing, even life for evermore." Psalm 133.

Or the following may be sung :

Music—*"Auld Lang Syne,"* or *"Arlington."*

Behold how pleasant and how good,
   For brethren such as we, .
Of the Accepted brotherhood,
   To dwell in unity !

'Tis like oil on Aaron's head
   Which to his feet distils,
Like Hermon's dew so richly shed
   On Zion's sacred hills.

For there the Lord of Light and Love,
   A blessing sent with pow'r :
Oh ! may we all this blessing prove
   E'en life for evermore.

On Friendship's altar rising here,
   Our hands now plighted be
To live in love with hearts sincere,
   In peace and unity.

*   *   *   *   *   *   *

"In the beginning God created the heaven and the earth. And the earth was without form and void ; and darkness was upon the face of the deep. And the Spirit of God moved upon the face of the waters. And God said, Let there be light : and there was light." * * * *

THE SHOCK OF ENLIGHTENMENT.

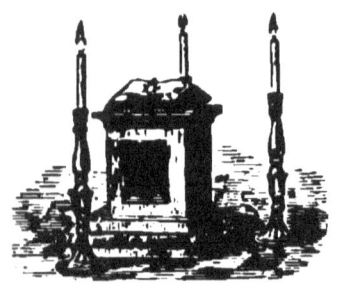

The Holy Bible is given us as the rule and guide of faith ; the Square to square our actions ; and the Compasses to circumscribe and keep us within due bounds with all mankind, but more especially with the brethren in Masonry.

   *   *   *   *   *   *   *

As the sun rules the day, and the moon governs the night, so should the W. M. endeavor to rule and govern the Lodge with equal regularity.

   *   *   *   *   *   *   *

THE APRON.

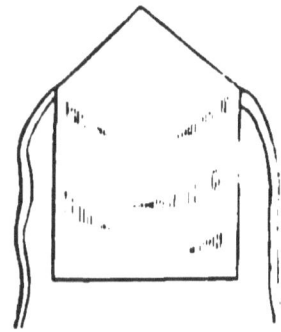

I now present you the lambskin or white leather

apron, which is an emblem of innocence, and the
badge of a Mason, more ancient than the Golden
Fleece or Roman Eagle; more honorable than
the Star and Garter, or any other order that can
be conferred upon you at this time, or any future
period, by king, prince, potentate, or any other
person, except he be a Mason, and which I hope
you will wear with equal pleasure to yourself, and
honor to the fraternity.

Or the following symbolism of the Apron, by W. Bro.
Robert F. Stobo, of New York, may be used with good
effect:

MY BROTHER :—I now present you this lambskin
or white leather apron. It is an emblem of innocence and the *distinguished* badge of a Mason.

It may be that, in coming years, upon your
head shall rest the laurel leaves of victory; on
your breast may hang jewels fit to grace the dia-
dem of an Eastern potentate; nay, more than
these, with light added to the coming light, your
ambitious feet may tread round after round the
ladder that leads to fame in our mystic circle, and
even the purple of our fraternity may rest upon
your honored shoulders; but never again from
mortal hands never again, until your enfranchised
spirit shall have passed upward and inward
through the pearly gates, shall any honor so dis-

tinguished, so emblematic of purity and all per-
fections, be bestowed upon you as this which I
now confer. It is yours to wear throughout an
honorable life, and at your death to be placed
upon the coffin which shall contain your earthly
remains, and with them laid beneath the silent
clods of the valley.

Let its pure and spotless surface be to you an
ever-present reminder of a "purity of life and
rectitude of conduct," a never-ending argument
for nobler deeds, for higher thoughts, for greater
achievements. And when at last your weary feet
shall have come to the end of their toilsome journey, and from your nerveless grasp shall drop for-
ever the working tools of life, may the record of
your life and actions be as pure and spotless as
the fair emblem which I place within your hands
to-night. And when your trembling soul shall
stand naked and alone before the Great White
Throne, may it be your portion to hear from Him
who sitteth as the Judge Supreme the welcome
words—" Well done, good and faithful servant;
enter thou into the joy of thy Lord."

THE DEMAND.

NORTH EAST CORNER.

THE WORKING TOOLS.

The working tools of an Entered Apprentice are the *Twenty-four inch Gauge*, and the *Common Gavel.*

The *twenty-four inch gauge* is an instrument used by operative masons to measure and lay out their work, but we, as Free and Accepted Masons, are taught to make use of it for the noble and glorious purpose of dividing our time. It being divided into twenty-four equal parts, is emblematic of the twenty-four hours of the day, which we are taught to divide into three equal parts ; whereby are found eight hours for the service of God, and a distressed worthy brother ; eight for our usual avocations ; and eight for refreshment and sleep.

The *common gavel* is an instrument made use of by operative masons to break off the corners of rough stones, the better to fit them for the builder's use ; but we, as Free and Accepted Masons, are taught to make use of it for the more noble and glorious purpose of divesting our hearts and consciences of all the vices and superfluities of life, thereby fitting our minds as living stones for that spiritual building, " that house not made with hands, eternal in the heavens."

SECOND SECTION.

PREPARATION.

There is much analogy between the preparation of the candidate in Masonry, and the preparation for entering the Temple, as practised among the ancient Israelites. The Talmudical treatise, entitled " Beracoth," prescribes the regulation in these words : " No man shall enter the Lord's house with his staff (an offensive weapon), nor with his outer garment, nor with his shoes on his feet, nor with money in his purse."

Various passages of Scripture are referred to in this section, as elucidating the traditions of Masonry on the subject of the Temple.

"And the house when it was in building, was built of stone made ready before it was brought thither : so that there was neither hammer, nor axe, nor any tool of iron heard in the house, while it was in building." 1 Kings vi. 7.

"And we will cut wood out of Lebanon, as much as thou shalt need ; and we will bring it to thee in floats by sea to Joppa ; and thou shalt carry it up to Jerusalem." 2 Chron. ii. 16.

Josephus says : " The whole structure of the Temple was made with great skill, of polished stones, and those laid together so very harmoniously and smoothly, that there appeared to the spectators no sign of any hammer or other instrument of architecture, but as if, without any use of them, the entire materials had naturally united themselves together, so that the agreement of one part with another seemed rather to have been natural, than to have arisen from the force of tools upon them."

Masonry regards no man for his worldly wealth or honors ; it is therefore the internal and not the external qualifications which recommend a man to Masons.

"Now this was the manner in former time in Israel concerning redeeming and concerning changing, for to confirm all things, a man plucked off his shoe, and gave it to his neighbor, and this was a testimony in Israel." Ruth iv. 7.

In the ancient mysteries the aspirant was always kept for a certain period in a condition of darkness. Hence darkness became the symbolism of initiation. Applied to Masonic symbolism, it is intended to remind the candidate of his ignorance, which Masonry is to enlighten ; of his evil nature, which Masonry is to purify ; of the world, in whose obscurity he has been wandering, and from which Masonry is to rescue him.

"Ask, and it shall be given you ; seek, and ye shall find ; knock, and it shall be opened unto you."

In the ancient initiations, the candidate was never permitted on the threshold of the temple or sacred cavern, in which the ceremonies were conducted, until by the most solemn warning he had been impressed with the necessity of caution, secrecy, and fortitude.

No man should enter upon any great or important undertaking, without first invoking the blessing of Deity.

TRUST IN GOD!

This constitutes the sole creed of a Mason—at least, the only creed he is required to profess.

* * * * * * *

THE LEFT SIDE.

* * * * * * *

THE RIGHT HAND.

The right was by our ancient brethren esteemed the seat of fidelity; sometimes represented by two right hands joined; at others by two human figures, holding each other by the right hand.

THE BADGE OF A MASON.

The lamb has in all ages been deemed an emblem of *innocence*; he, therefore, who wears the lambskin as the badge of a Mason, is thereby continually reminded of that purity of life and conduct, so essentially necessary to his gaining admission into the Celestial Lodge above, where the Supreme Architect of the Universe presides.

THE LESSON OF CHARITY.

This is among the first lessons we are taught, when we pass the threshold of the mystic temple.

THE FIRST INSTRUCTIONS.

The candidate now receives the first instructions, upon which to build his future moral and Masonic edifice.

THIRD SECTION.

This section explains what constitutes and what authorizes a Masonic Lodge; where held, its form, support, covering, furniture, ornaments, lights and jewels, how situated, and to whom dedicated.

A Lodge is a certain number of Masons duly assembled, having the Holy Bible, Square and Compasses, and a Charter or Warrant empowering them to work.

WHERE LODGES ARE HELD.

Our ancient brethren held their Lodges on high hills, or in low dells, the better to observe cowans and eaves-droppers.

THE FORM OF A LODGE.

The form of a Lodge is an oblong, extending from East to West, between North and South, from its surface to its center, and from earth to heaven ; and is (symbolically said to be) of such vast dimensions, to denote the universality of Masonry, and that a Mason's charity should be equally extensive. A Masonic Lodge is a symbol of the world.

THE SUPPORTS OF A LODGE.

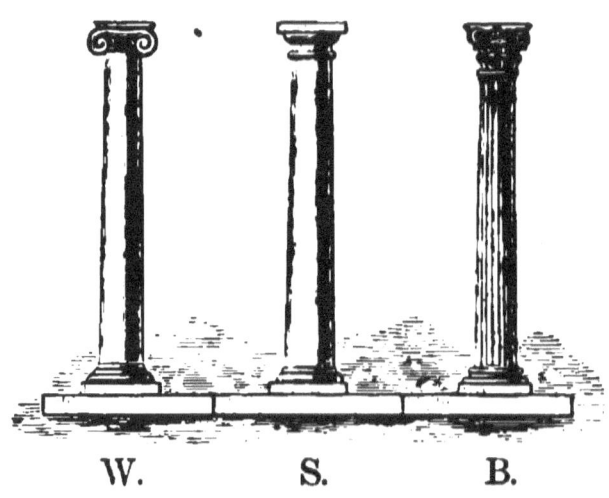

W.　　　　S.　　　　B.

This vast fabric is supported by three great pillars, denominated *Wisdom, Strength,* and *Beauty;* because it is necessary there should be wisdom to contrive, strength to support, and beauty to adorn all great and important undertakings. The W. M. represents the pillar of wisdom, it being supposed that he has wisdom * * * *. The S. W. represents the pillar of strength, it being his duty

to assist * * * *. The J. W. represents the pillar
of beauty, it being his duty to observe * * * *.

THE COVERING OF A LODGE.

The covering of a Lodge is a clouded canopy
or starry decked heaven, where all good Masons
hope at last to arrive, by aid of the theological
ladder which Jacob in his vision saw extending
from earth to heaven ; the three principal rounds
of which are denominated *Faith, Hope,* and *Charity;* and which admonish us to have faith in God,
hope in immortality, and charity to all mankind ;
of these the greatest is charity ; faith may be lost
in sight, hope ends in fruition, but charity extends
beyond the grave through the boundless realms.
of eternity.

THE FURNITURE OF A LODGE.

The furniture of a Lodge consists of the *Holy Bible, Square,* and *Compasses;* the Holy Bible is dedicated to God, as the inestimable gift of God to man, and * * * * ; the Square to the Master, it being the proper Masonic emblem of his office; and the Compasses to the Craft, because by a due attention to their use, they are taught to circumscribe their desires, and keep their passions within due bounds.

THE ORNAMENTS OF A LODGE.

The ornaments of a Lodge are the *mosaic pave-ment, indented tessel*, and *blazing star;* the mosaic pavement is a representation of the ground floor of King Solomon's Temple; the indented tessel, that beautiful border or skirting which surrounded it. The mosaic pavement is emblematic of human life checkered with good and evil; the beautiful border which surrounds it, the blessing and comforts which surround us, and which we hope to obtain by a faithful reliance on divine providence, which is hieroglyphically represented in the blazing star in the center.

THE LIGHTS OF A LODGE.

A Lodge has *three lights* situated East, West, and South, but none in the North. King Solomon's Temple was situated so far North of the ecliptic, that neither the sun or moon at meridian, could dart any rays into the northern part thereof; the North is therefore Masonically termed a place of darkness.

THE JEWELS OF A LODGE.

A Lodge has *six jewels, three immovable* and *three movable;* the immovable jewels are the *Square, Level,* and *Plumb;* the square inculcates morality, the level equality, and the plumb rectitude of life.

The *movable jewels* are the *rough ashlar*, the *perfect ashlar*, and the *trestle-board*. The rough ashlar is a stone as taken from the quarry in its rude and natural state; the perfect ashlar is a stone made ready by the hands of the workman, to be adjusted by the tools of the Fellow-Craft; the trestle-board is for the master-workman to draw his designs upon. By the rough ashlar we are reminded of our rude and imperfect state by nature; by the perfect ashlar that state of perfection, at which we hope to arrive, by a virtuous education, our own endeavors, and the blessing of God. By the trestle-board we are also reminded, that as the operative workman erects his temporal building agreeably to the rules and designs laid down by the master on the trestle-board, so should we, both operative and speculative, endeavor to erect our spiritual building agreeably to the rules and designs laid down by the Supreme Architect of the Universe, in the great books of nature and revelation, which are our spiritual, moral, and Masonic trestle-board.

SITUATION OF LODGES.

Lodges are situated due *East* and *West*, that being the situation of King Solomon's Temple. After Moses had safely conducted the children of Israel through the Red Sea, into the wilderness, when pursued by Pharaoh and his host, he there, by divine command, erected a tabernacle due East and West, in order to perpetuate the remembrance of that mighty East wind, by which their miraculous deliverance was wrought, and also to receive the rays of the rising sun. This

was an exact model of King Solomon's Temple,
for which reason Lodges are so situated.

TO WHOM DEDICATED.

Lodges were anciently dedicated to King Solomon, who was our first Most Excellent Grand
Master, but modern Masons dedicate theirs to
Saint John the Baptist, and Saint John the Evan-
gelist, who were two eminent patrons of Masonry,
and since their time there is represented in every
regular and well-governed Lodge, a certain point
within a circle, embordered by two perpendicular
parallel lines, representing those two Saints, and
upon the top rest the Holy Scriptures, which
point out the whole duty of man; the point representing an individual brother; the circle the
boundary line of his duty to God and man, beyond which he is never to suffer his passions,
prejudices, or interests to betray him on any occasion.   In going round this circle we necessarily

touch upon these two lines, as well as upon the
Holy Scriptures, and while a Mason keeps him-
self thus circumscribed, it is impossible that he
should materially err.

TENETS.

The tenets of a Mason's profession are

BROTHERLY LOVE, RELIEF, AND TRUTH.

BROTHERLY LOVE.

By the exercise of brotherly love
we are taught to regard the whole
human species—the high and low,
the rich and poor—as one family;
who, as created by one Almighty
parent, and inhabitants of the same planet, are
to aid, support, and protect each other. On this
principle Masonry unites men of every country,
sect, and opinion, and conciliates true friendship
among those, who otherwise might have remained
at a perpetual distance.

RELIEF.

To relieve the distressed is a duty
incumbent on all men, but particularly on Masons, who are linked together by an indissoluble chain of
sincere affection. To soothe the un-
happy, to sympathize with their misfortunes, to

compassionate their miseries, and to restore peace
to their troubled minds, is the great aim we have
in view. On this basis we form our friendships
and establish our connections.

TRUTH.

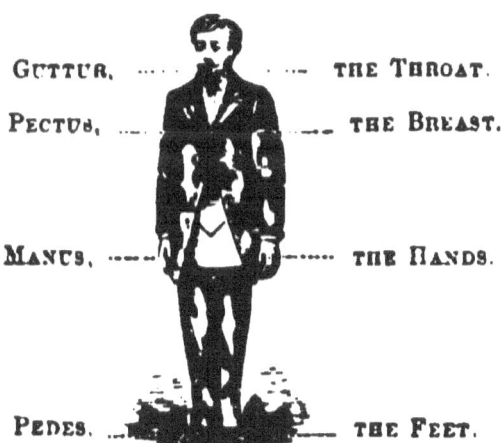

Truth is a divine attribute and
the foundation of every virtue. To
be good and true, is the first lesson
we are taught in Masonry. On this
theme we contemplate, and by its
dictates endeavor to regulate our conduct; hence,
while influenced by this principle, hypocrisy and
deceit are unknown among us, sincerity and plain-
dealing distinguish us, and the heart and tongue
join in promoting each other's welfare, and re-
joicing in each other's prosperity.

GUTTUR, ········ THE THROAT.

PECTUS, ········ THE BREAST.

MANUS, ········ THE HANDS.

PEDES, ········ THE FEET.

Every Mason has four * * * *, which are

illustrated by the four cardinal virtues, *Temperance*, *Fortitude*, *Prudence*, and *Justice*, and are thus explained:

TEMPERANCE.

EMPERANCE is that due restraint upon our affections and passions which renders the body tame and governable, and frees the mind from the allurements of vice. This virtue should be the constant practice of every Mason, as he is thereby taught to avoid excess or contracting any licentious or vicious habit, the indulgence of which might lead him to disclose some of those valuable secrets which he has promised to conceal and never reveal, and which would consequently subject him to the contempt and detestation of all good Masons * * * * †.

FORTITUDE.

ORTITUDE is that noble and steady purpose of the mind whereby we are enabled to undergo any pain, peril, or danger when prudentially deemed expedient. This virtue is equally distant from rashness and cowardice ; and, like the former, should be deeply impressed upon the mind of every Mason, as a safeguard or security against any illegal attack that may be made by force or otherwise, to extort from him any of those valuable secrets with which he has been so solemnly intrusted, and which were emblematically represented upon his first admission into the Lodge * * * * † †.

PRUDENCE.

RUDENCE teaches to regulate our lives and actions agreeably to the dictates of reason, and is that habit by which we wisely judge and prudentially determine on all things relative to our present as well as to our future happiness. This virtue should be the peculiar characteristic of every Mason, not only for the government of his conduct while in the Lodge, but also when abroad in the world. It should be particularly attended to in all strange and mixed companies, never to let fall the least sign, token, or word whereby the secrets of Masonry might be unlawfully obtained * * * * † † †.

JUSTICE.

USTICE is that standard, or boundary of right, which enables us to render to every man his just due, without distinction. This virtue is not only consistent with Divine and human laws, but is the very cement and support of civil society; and as justice in

a great measure constitutes the real good man, so
should it be the invariable practice of every Mason never to deviate from the minutest principles
thereof * * * * † † † †.

Entered Apprentices should serve their masters
with freedom, fervency, and zeal, which are represented by

There is nothing more zealous than Clay or
Mother Earth, for it is that alone, of all the ele-
ments, which has never proved unfriendly to man;
bodies of water deluge him with rain, oppress
him with hail, and drown him with inundation.
The air rushes in storms, prepares the tempest,
and fire lights up the volcano; but the earth, ever
kind and indulgent, is found subservient to his
wishes.   Though constantly harassed, more to
furnish the luxuries than the necessaries of life,
she never refuses her accustomed yield ; spreading
his pathway with flowers and his table with plenty; though she produces poison, still she supplies
the antidote, and returns with interest every good
committed to her care; and when at last we are

called upon to pass through the "dark valley of the shadow of Death," she once more receives us, and piously covers our remains within her bosom, thus admonishing us, that as from it we came, so to it we must shortly return.

CHARGE AT INITIATING INTO THE DEGREE OF ENTERED APPRENTICE.

BROTHER:—As you are now introduced into the first principles of Masonry, I congratulate you upon being accepted into this ancient and honorable Order ; ancient, as having existed from time immemorial ; and honorable, as tending in every particular, so to render all men who will be conformable to its precepts. No institution was ever raised on a better principle or more solid foundations ; nor were ever more excellent rules and useful maxims laid down than are inculcated in the several Masonic lectures. The greatest and best men in all ages have been promoters and encouragers of the art, and have never deemed it derogatory to their dignity to level themselves with the fraternity, extend their privileges, and patronize their assemblies. There are three great duties, which, as a Mason, you are charged to inculcate—to God, your neighbor, and yourself. To God, in never mentioning his name but with that reverential awe which is due from a creature to his Creator ; in imploring his aid in all your laudable undertakings, and in esteeming him as the chief good ; to your neighbor, in acting upon the square, and doing unto him as you wish he would do unto you ; and to yourself, in avoiding all irregularity and intemperance, which may impair your faculties, or debase the dignity of your profession. The performance of these duties will entitle you to public and private esteem.

In the State you are to be a quiet and peaceable citizen, true to your government and just to your country. You are not to countenance disloyalty or rebellion, but patiently submit to legal authority, and conform with cheerfulness to the government of the country in which you live. In your outward demeanor, be particularly careful to avoid censure or reproach.

Although your frequent appearance at our regular meetings is earnestly solicited, yet it is not meant that Masonry should interfere with your necessary vocations, for these are on no account to be neglected; neither are you to suffer your zeal for the institution to lead you into argument with those who, through ignorance, may ridicule it.

During your leisure hours, that you may improve in Masonic knowledge, you are to converse with well-informed brethren, who will always be as ready to give, as you will be to receive, instruction.

Finally, keep sacred and inviolable the mysteries of the Order, as these are to distinguish you from the rest of the community, and mark your consequence among Masons. If in the circle of your acquaintance, you find a person desirous of being initiated into Masonry, be particularly attentive not to recommend him unless you are convinced he will conform to our rules ; that the honor, glory, and reputation of the institution may be firmly established, and the world at large convinced of its good effects.

FELLOW CRAFT'S DEGREE.

This degree is divided into two sections. While it extends the plan of knowledge commenced in the first degree, it comprehends a more extensive system of learning, and inculcates, in our peculiar method, the most important truths of science.

FIRST SECTION.

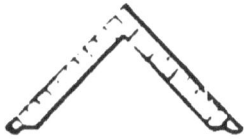

The square as a symbol, is peculiarly appropriated to this degree. It is intended to teach the Fellow Craft that the square of virtue should be a rule and guide to his conduct, in all his future transactions with mankind.

*   *   *   *   *   *   *

"Thus he showed me; and the Lord stood upon a wall made by a plumb-line, with a plumb-line in his hand. And the Lord said unto me, Amos, what seest thou? And I said, a plumb-line. Then said the Lord, Behold, I will set a plumb-line in the midst of my people Israel: I will not again pass by them any more." Amos vii. 7, 8

Or the following Ode may be sung:

Music—"*Portuguese Hymn.*"—11s.

Come, Craftsmen, assembled our pleasures to share,
Who walk by the Plumb, and work by the Square,
While traveling in love on the Level of time,
Sweet hope shall light on to a far better clime.

We'll seek in our labors the Spirit Divine,
Our temple to bless and our hearts to refine,
And thus to our altar a tribute will bring,
While joined in true friendship our anthem we sing.

See Order and Beauty rise gently to view,
Each Brother a column, so perfect and true;
When Orders shall cease, and Temples decay,
May each fairer columns immortal survey.

*   *   *   *   *   *   *

THE WORKING TOOLS.

 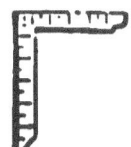 

The working tools of a Feilow Craft are the *Plumb*, the *Square*, and the *Level*.

The Plumb is an instrument made use of by operative masons to raise perpendiculars, the Square to square their work, and the Level to lay horizontals ; but we, as Free and Accepted Masons, are taught to make use of them for more noble and glorious purposes ; the plumb admonishes us to walk uprightly in our several stations before God and man, squaring our actions by the square of virtue, and remembering that we are traveling upon the level of time to that undiscovered country, from whose bourne no traveler returns.

SECOND SECTION.

PREPARATION FOR ADVANCEMENT.

*   *   *   *   *   *   *

ADMISSION.

The Attentive Ear.   The Instructive Tongue.   The Faithful Breast.

*   *   *   *   *   *   *

THE SQUARE OF VIRTUE.

*   *   *   *   *   *   *

Masonry is considered under two denominations, *Operative* and *Speculative*.

OPERATIVE MASONRY.

By operative Masonry we allude to a proper application of the useful rules of architecture, whence a structure will derive figure, strength, and beauty, and whence will result a due proportion, and a just correspondence in all its parts. It furnishes us with dwellings, and with convenient shelters from the vicissitudes and inclemencies of the seasons, and while it displays the effects of human wisdom, as well in the choice as in the arrangement of the sundry materials of which an edifice is composed, it demonstrates that a fund of science and industry is implanted in man for the best, most salutary, and beneficent purposes.

SPECULATIVE MASONRY.

By speculative Masonry we learn to subdue the passions, act upon the square, keep a tongue of good report, maintain secrecy, and practice charity. It is so far interwoven with religion, as to lay us under obligation to pay that rational homage to the Deity which at once constitutes our duty and our happiness. It leads the contemplative Mason to view with reverence and admiration the glorious works of creation, and inspires him with the most exalted ideas of the perfection of his Divine Creator.

* * * * for in six days God created the heaven
and the earth, and rested upon the seventh day ;
the seventh, therefore, our ancient brethren con-
secrated as a day of rest from their labors ; thereby
enjoying frequent opportunities to contemplate
the glorious works of creation, and to adore their
great Creator.

THE PILLARS OF THE PORCH.

"Also he made before the house two pillars of
thirty and five cubits high, and the chapiter that
was on the top of each of them was five cubits."
2 Chron. iii. 15.

PEACE, UNITY, AND PLENTY.

THE GLOBES.

The globes are two artificial and spherical bodies on the convex surface of which are represented the countries, seas, and various parts of the earth; the face of the heavens, the planetary revolutions and other particulars.

THE USE OF THE GLOBES.

Their principal use, besides serving as maps to distinguish the outward parts of the earth, and the situation of the fixed stars, is to illustrate and explain the phenomena arising from the annual revolution and the diurnal rotation of the earth around its own axis. They are the noblest instruments for improving the mind, and giving it the most distinct idea of any problem or proposition, as well as enabling it to solve the same. Contemplating these bodies, we are inspired with a due reverence for the Deity and his works, and are induced to encourage the studies of astronomy,

geography, and navigation, and the arts depend-
ent on them, by which society has been so much
benefited.   They further denote the universality
of Masonry.

*   *   *

*   *   *   *   *

ORDER IN ARCHITECTURE.

By order in architecture is meant a system of
all the members, proportions, and ornaments of
columns and pilasters; or it is a regular arrangement of the projecting parts of a building, which,
united with those of a column, form a beautiful,
perfect, and complete whole.

ITS ANTIQUITY.

From the first formation of society order in
architecture may be traced.   When the rigor of
seasons obliged men to contrive shelter from the
inclemency of the weather, we learn that they first
planted trees on end, and then laid others across,
to support a covering.   The bands which connected
these trees at top and bottom, are said to have
given rise to the idea of the base and capital of
pillars; and from this simple hint originally pro-
ceeded the more improved art of architecture.

The five orders are thus classed : the *Ionic,
Doric, Corinthian, Tuscan,* and *Composite.*   Of

these the ones most esteemed by Masons are the ancient and original orders which are no more than three, the Ionic, Doric, and Corinthian, which were invented by the Greeks. To these, the Romans have added·two, the Tuscan and the Composite. To the Greeks therefore, and not to the Romans, are we indebted for what is great, judicious, and distinct in architecture.

* * * * * to the five senses ·of Human Nature, *Hearing, Seeing, Feeling, Smelling,* and *Tasting.* Of these, the ones most esteemed by Masons are Hearing, Seeing, and Feeling, for by * * * *.

* * * * * * * to the seven Liberal Arts and Sciences which are *Grammar, Rhetoric, Logic, Arithmetic, Geometry, Music,* and *Astronomy ;* of these the one most esteemed by Masons is Geometry, or the fifth science.

GEOMETRY

treats of the powers and properties of magnitudes in general, where length, breadth, and thickness are considered, from a point to a line, from a line to a superfices, from a superfices to a solid.

A point is a dimensionless figure, or an indivisible part of space.

A line is a point continued, and a figure of one capacity, namely, length.

A superfices is a figure of two dimensions, namely, length and breadth.

A solid is a figure of three dimensions, namely, length, breadth, and thickness.

THE ADVANTAGES OF GEOMETRY.

By this science the architect is enabled to construct his plans and execute his designs ; the general, to arrange his soldiers ; the geographer, to give us the dimensions of the world, and all things therein contained ; to delineate the extent of seas, and specify the divisions of empires, kingdoms, and provinces. By it, also, the astronomer is enabled to make his observations, and to fix the duration of time and seasons, years and cycles.

In fine, geometry is the foundation of architecture, and the root of mathematics.

Astronomy also claims our attention :

ASTRONOMY

is that divine art by which we are taught to read the wisdom, strength, and beauty of the Almighty Creator in those sacred pages, the celestial hemisphere.

Assisted by astronomy, we can observe the magnitudes, and calculate the period and eclipses of the heavenly bodies. By it we learn the use of the globes, the system of the world, and the preliminary laws of nature. While we are employed

in the study of this science, we must perceive un-
paralleled instances of wisdom and goodness ;
and through the whole creation, trace the glorious
Author by his works.

*　　*　　*　　*　　*　　*　　*

G

THE MORAL ADVANTAGES OF GEOMETRY.

Geometry, the first and noblest of sciences, i
the basis on which the superstructure of Masonry
is erected.　By geometry, we may curiously trace
Nature, through her various windings, to her most
concealed recesses.　By it we may discover the
power, the wisdom, and the goodness of the Grand
Artificer of the Universe, and view with delight
the proportions which connect this vast machine.

By it we may discover how the planets move in
their different orbits, and demonstrate their various revolutions.　By it we account for the return
of seasons, and the variety of scenes which each
season displays to the discerning eye.　Number-
less worlds are around us, all framed by the same
Divine Artist, which roll through the vast expanse,
and are all conducted by the same unerring law
of Nature.

A survey of Nature, and the observation of her
beautiful proportions, first determined man to

imitate the Divine plan, and study symmetry and order. This gave rise to societies, and birth to every useful art. The architect began to design, and the plans which he laid down, being improved by experience and time, have produced works which are the admiration of every age.

The lapse of time, the ruthless hand of ignorance, and the devastations of war, have laid waste and destroyed many valuable monuments of antiquity, on which the utmost exertions of human genius have been employed. Even the Temple of Solomon, so spacious and magnificent, and constructed by so many celebrated artists, escaped not the unsparing ravages of barbarous force. Freemasonry, notwithstanding, has still survived. The *attentive ear* receives the sound from the *instructive tongue*, and the secrets of Freemasonry are safely lodged in the repository of *faithful breasts*. Tools and implements of architecture, and symbolic emblems most expressive, are selected by the Fraternity to imprint upon the mind wise and serious truths ; and thus through a succession of ages, are transmitted unimpaired the most excellent tenets of our institution.

O   O   O

The lecture closes by paying profound homage to the Grand Geometrician of the Universe, before whom all Masons, from the youngest E. A. to the W. M., who presides in the East, should with reverence most humbly bow

CHARGE AT PASSING TO THE DEGREE OF FELLOW CRAFT.

BROTHER:—Being passed to the second degree of Masonry, we congratulate you on your preferment. The internal, and not the external qualifications of a man, are what Masonry regards. As you increase in knowledge, you will improve in social intercourse.

It is unnecessary to recapitulate the duties which as a Mason you are bound to discharge, or enlarge on the necessity of a strict adherence to them, as your own experience must have established their value. Our laws and regulations you are strenuously to support, and be always ready to assist in seeing them duly executed. You are not to palliate or aggravate the offences of your brethren; but in the decision of every trespass against our rules, you are to judge with candor, admonish with friendship, and reprehend with justice.

The study of the liberal arts, that valuable branch of education which tends so effectually to polish and adorn the mind, is earnestly recommended to your consideration; especially the science of geometry, which is established as the basis of our art. Geometry, or Masonry, originally synonymous terms, being of a divine and moral nature, is enriched with the most useful knowledge; while it proves the wonderful properties of nature, it demonstrates the more important truths of morality.

Your past behavior and regular deportment have merited the honor which we have now conferred; and in your new character it is expected that you will conform to the principles of the Order, by steadily persevering in the practice of every commendable virtue. Such is the nature of your engagement as a Fellow Craft, and to these duties you are bound by the most sacred ties.

MASTER MASON'S DEGREE.

This has very properly been called the *sublime degree of a Master Mason*, as well, for the solemnity of the ceremonies which accompany it, as the profound lessons of wisdom which it inculcates. The important part of the degree is to symbolize the great doctrines of the resurrection of the body and the immortality of the soul; and hence it has been remarked by a learned writer of our Order that "the Master Mason represents a man saved from the grave of iniquity, and raised to the faith of salvation." The lecture is divided into three sections.

FIRST SECTION.

The Compasses are peculiarly dedicated to this degree, because between their extreme points when properly extended, are emblematically said to be contained the jewels of a Master Mason, which are *Friendship, Morality,* and *Brotherly Love.*

*   *   *   *   *   *   *

"Remember now thy Creator in the days of thy youth, while the evil days come not, nor the years draw nigh when thou shalt say, I have no pleasure in them; while the sun, or the light, or the moon, or the stars, be not darkened, nor the clouds return after the rain; in the days when the keepers of the house shall tremble, and the strong men shall bow themselves, and the grinders cease because they are few, and those that look out of the window be darkened, and the doors shall be shut in the streets; when the sound of the grinding is low, and he shall rise up at the voice of the bird, and all the daughters of music shall be brought low; also when they shall be afraid of that which is high, and fears shall be in the way, and the almond tree shall flourish, and the grasshopper shall be a burden, and desire shall fail: because man goeth to his long home, and the mourners go about the streets : or ever the silver cord be loosed, or the golden bowl be broken, or the pitcher be broken at the fountain, or the wheel broken at the cistern.   Then shall the dust return to the earth as it was: and the spirit shall return to God who gave it."   Eccl. xii. 1–7.

Or the following O.le may be sung :

MUSIC—*"Bonny Doon,"* or *"Hamburg."*—L. M.

> Let us remember in our youth
>> Before the evil day draws nigh,
> Our Great Creator and his Truth,
>> Ere memory fail and pleasure fly!

Or sun, or moon, or planet's light
   Grow dark, or clouds return in gloom!
Ere vital spark no more incite!
   When strength shall bow, and years consume.

Let us, in youth, remember Him
   Who formed our frame, and spirits gave,
Ere windows of the mind grow dim,
   Or door of speech obstructed wave!

When voice of bird fresh terrors wake,
   And Music's daughters charm no more,
Or fear to rise, with trembling shake,
   Along the path we travel o'er.

*   *   *   *   *   *   *

THE WORKING TOOLS.

The working tools of a Master Mason are all the implements of Masonry indiscriminately, but more especially the *Trowel.*

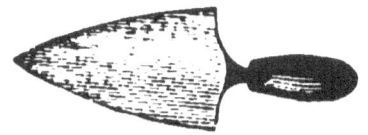

The Trowel is an instrument made use of by operative masons to spread the cement which unites a building into one common mass; but we, as Free and Accepted Masons, are taught to make use of it for the more noble and glorious purpose of spreading the cement of brotherly love and affection; that cement which unites us into one sacred band, or society of friends and brothers, among whom no contention should ever exist, but that noble contention, or rather emulation, of who can best work and best agree.

*   *   *   *   *   *   *

SECOND SECTION.

*   *   *   *   *   *   *

MUSIC—"*Pleyel's Hymn.*"—7s.

Solemn strikes the funeral chime,
Notes of our departing time,
As we journey here below,
Through a pilgrimage of woe.

Mortals, now indulge a tear,
For mortality is here,
See how wide her trophies wave
O'er the slumbers of the grave.

Here another guest we bring,
Seraphs of celestial wing,
To our funeral altar come;
Waft our friend and brother home.

Lord of all below, above,
Fill our souls with truth and love,

As dissolves our earthly tie,
Take us to thy Lodge on high.

Or the following may be used:

Hark! from the tombs a doleful sound,
  Mine ears attend the cry,
Ye living men, come view the ground
  Where shortly you must lie.

Princes, this clay must be your bed,
  In spite of all your towers;
The tall, the wise, the reverend head,
  Must lie as low as ours.

Great God, is this our certain doom?
  And are we still secure?
Still walking downward to the tomb,
  And yet prepare no more?

Grant us the power of quick'ning grace,
  To fit our souls to fly,
That when we drop this dying flesh,
  We'll rise above the sky.

*   *   *   *   *   *   *

The following prayer is prescribed for this section:

PRAYER.

" Thou, O God, knowest our down-sitting and our up-rising, and understandest our thoughts afar off. Shield and defend us from the evil intentions of our enemies, and support us under the trials and afflictions we are destined to endure while traveling through this vale of tears. Man that is born of a woman is of few days, and full of trouble. He cometh forth as a flower, and is cut down ; he fleeth as a shadow, and continueth not. Seeing his days are determined, the number of his months are with thee ; thou hast appointed his bounds that he cannot pass ; turn from him, that he may rest, till he shall accomplish his day. For there is hope of a tree, if it be cut down, that it will sprout again, and that the tender branch thereof will not cease. But man dieth and wasteth away ; yea, man giveth up the ghost, and where is he? As the waters fail from the sea, and the flood decayeth and drieth up, so man lieth down, and riseth not up until the heavens shall be no more. Yet, O Lord! have compassion on the children of thy creation, administer them comfort in time of trouble, and save them with an everlasting salvation."

"So mote it be.   Amen."

It has been the practice in all ages to erect monuments to the memory of departed worth.

THIRD SECTION.

The third section furnishes many details in relation to the Temple, and concludes with an explanation of the hieroglyphical emblems of the degree.

This vast fabric was founded in the fourth year of the reign of King Solomon, during the second month of the sacred year, on the hill of Mount Moriah, near the place where Abraham was about to offer up Isaac, and where David met and appeased the destroying angel.

It was supported by fourteen hundred and

fifty-three columns, and two thousand nine hundred and six pilasters, all hewn from the finest parian marble.

There are three grand Masonic pillars, denominated *Wisdom, Strength,* and *Beauty:* * * * *.

There were employed in building the Temple, three Grand Masters, three thousand and three hundred Overseers, or Masters of the work; eighty thousand Fellow Crafts, or hewers on the mountain, or in the quarry; and seventy thousand Entered Apprentices or bearers of burdens: these were all so classed and arranged by the wisdom of Solomon that neither envy, discord, or confusion was suffered to interrupt or disturb the peace and good-fellowship which prevailed among the workmen at this important period.

7⅙ G. F.   5⅔ M. C.   3 S. S.

There are in this degree two classes of emblems or symbols, the first of which is monitorial, and consists of the *Pot of Incense*, the *Bee-Hive*, the *Book of Constitutions, guarded by the Tiler's Sword*, the *Sword pointing to a naked heart*, the *All-Seeing Eye*, the *Anchor* and *Ark*, the *Forty-seventh problem of Euclid*, the *Hour-Glass*, the *Three Steps* and the *Scythe*, and are thus explained :

THE POT OF INCENSE

is an emblem of a pure heart, which is always an acceptable sacrifice to the Deity ; and as this glows with fervent heat, so should our hearts continually glow with gratitude to the great and beneficent Author of our existence, for the manifold blessings and comforts we enjoy.

THE BEE-HIVE

is an emblem of industry, and recommends the practice of that virtue to all created beings, from the highest seraph in heaven to the lowest reptile of the dust. It teaches us, that as we came into the world rational and intelligent beings, so should we be industrious ones; never sitting down contented while our fellow-creatures around us are in want, when it is in our power to relieve them without inconvenience to ourselves.

THE BOOK OF CONSTITUTIONS, GUARDED BY THE TILER'S SWORD,

reminds us that we should be ever watchful and guarded in our words and actions, particularly when before the enemies of Masonry; ever bearing in remembrance those truly Masonic virtues, silence and circumspection.

THE SWORD POINTING TO A NAKED HEART

demonstrates that justice will sooner or later overtake us; and although our thoughts, words, and actions may be hidden from the eyes of man, yet that

ALL-SEEING EYE

whom the *Sun*, *Moon*, and *Stars* obey, and under whose watchful care even *Comets* perform their stupendous revolutions, pervades the utmost re-

cesses of the human *Heart*, and will reward us according to our merits.

THE ANCHOR AND ARK

are emblems of a well-grounded hope and a well-spent life. They are emblematic of that divine *Ark* which safely wafts us over this tempestuous sea of troubles, and that *Anchor* which shall safely moor us in a peaceful harbor, where the wicked cease from troubling, and the weary shall find rest.

THE FORTY-SEVENTH PROBLEM OF EUCLID.

 This was an invention of our ancient friend and brother Pythagoras, who, in his travels through Asia, Africa, and Europe, was initiated into several orders of priesthood, and raised to the sublime degree of Master Mason. This wise philosopher enriched his mind abundantly in a general knowledge of things, and more especially in Geometry or Masonry. On this subject he drew out many problems and theorems; and among the most distinguished he erected this, when in the joy of his heart, he exclaimed *Eureka*, in the Grecian language, signifying *I have found it;* and upon the discovery of which he is said to have sacrificed a hecatomb. It teaches Masons to be general lovers of the arts and sciences.

THE HOUR-GLASS

 is an emblem of human life. Behold! how swiftly the sands run, and how rapidly our lives are drawing to a close! We cannot without astonishment behold the little particles which are contained in this machine; how they pass away almost imperceptibly; and yet, to our surprise, in the short space of an hour they are all exhausted. Thus wastes man! To-day, he puts forth the tender

leaves of hope ; to-morrow, blossoms and bears his blushing honors thick upon him; the next day comes a frost which nips the shoot ; and when he thinks his greatness is still aspiring, he falls, like autumn leaves, to enrich our mother earth.

THE THREE STEPS,

usually delineated upon the Master's carpet, are emblematic of the three principal stages of human life, viz.: *Youth, Manhood*, and *Age.* In *Youth*, as Entered Apprentices, we ought industriously to occupy our minds in the attainment of useful knowledge ; in *Manhood*, as Fellow Crafts, we should apply our knowledge to the discharge of our respective duties to God, our neighbor, and ourselves; so that in *Age*, as Master Masons, we may enjoy the happy reflections consequent on a well-spent life, and die in the hope of a glorious immortality.

THE SCYTHE

is an emblem of time, which cuts the brittle thread of life, and launches us into eternity. Behold! what havoc the scythe of Time makes among the human race! If by chance we should escape the numerous evils incident to childhood and youth, and with health and vigor arrive at the years of manhood; yet, withal, we must soon be cut down by the all-devouring scythe of Time, and be gathered into the land where our fathers have gone before us.

The second class of emblems are not monitorial and therefore their true interpretation can only be obtained within the tiled recesses of the Lodge. They consist of the *Setting Maul*, the *Spade*, the *Coffin*, and the *Sprig of Acacia.*

Then   *   *   let us imitate the example of *   *   whom you have this evening represented, in his virtuous and amiable conduct, his un-feigned piety to God, and his inflexible fidelity to his trust, that we may welcome the grim tyrant Death, and receive him as a kind messenger sent from our Supreme Grand Master, to translate us from this imperfect, to that all-perfect, glorious, and celestial Lodge above, where the Supreme Architect of the Universe presides.

CHARGE AT RAISING TO THE SUBLIME DEGREE OF A MASTER MASON.

BROTHER:—Your zeal for the institution of Masonry, the progress you have made in the mysteries, and your conformity to our regulations, have pointed you out as a proper object of our favor and esteem. You are now bound by duty, honor, and gratitude to be faithful to your trust; to support the dignity of your character on every occasion; and to enforce, by precept and example, obedience to the tenets of the Order.

In the character of a Master Mason, you are authorized to correct the errors and irregularities of your uninformed brethren, and to guard them against a breach of fidelity. To preserve the reputation of the fraternity unsullied, must be your constant care; and for this purpose it is your province to recommend to your inferiors, obedience and submission; to your equals, courtesy and affability; to your superiors, kindness and condescension. Universal benevolence you are always to inculcate, and by the regularity of your own behavior afford the best example for the conduct of others less informed. The ancient landmarks of the Order intrusted to your care, you are carefully to preserve, and never suffer them to be infringed, or countenance a deviation from the established usages and customs of the fraternity.

Your virtue, honor, and reputation are concerned in supporting with dignity the character you now bear. Let no motive, therefore, make you swerve from your duty, violate your vows, or betray your trust; but be true and faithful, and imitate the example of that celebrated artist whom you have this evening represented. Thus you will render yourself deserving of the honor which we have conferred, and merit the confidence that we have reposed.

*   *   *   *   *   *   *

BY-LAWS.

*   *   *   *   *

FUNERAL SERVICES.

[For full directions, which are to be read to the brethren after the Lodge is opened, see Masonic Code of N. C.]

The brethren being assembled at the Lodge room (or some other convenient place) the Master opens the Lodge on the Third degree of Masonry with the usual forms; and having stated the purpose of the communication, the service begins:

Master—" What man is he that liveth, and shall not see death? Shall he deliver his soul from the hand of the grave?"

Response—" Man walketh in a vain shadow; he heapeth up riches, and cannot tell who shall gather them."

Master—" When he dieth he shall carry nothing away; his glory shall not descend after him."

Response—" Naked he came into the world, and naked he must return."

Master—" The Lord gave, and the Lord hath taken away; blessed be the name of the Lord!"

The Master, then taking the *roll* on which has been inscribed the name, age, date of initiation or affiliation, date of death, or any matters that may be interesting to the brethren in the future, and having read the same aloud, shall say:

"Let us live and die like the righteous, that our last end may be like his!"

Response—"God is our God for ever and ever; he will be our guide even unto death!"

Master—"Almighty Father! into thy hands we leave with humble submission the soul of our deceased brother."

The brethren answer, giving [*] *funeral* grand honors three times.

The first and second times:

"The will of God is accomplished! So mote it be. Amen."

The third time:

"We cherish his memory here. We commend his spirit to God who gave it. And commit his body to the tomb."

The Master then deposits the roll in the *archives*, and repeats the following prayer:

"Most glorious God! author of all good, and giver of all mercy! pour down thy blessings upon us, and strengthen our solemn engagements with

---

[*] Both arms are crossed on the breast, the left uppermost, and the open palms of the hands sharply striking the shoulders; they are then raised above the head the palms striking each other, and then made to fall smartly upon the thighs.

ties of sincere affection! May the present instance of mortality remind us of our approaching fate, and draw our attention toward thee, the only refuge in time of need! that, when the awful moment shall arrive, that we are about to quit this transitory scene, the enlivening prospect of thy mercy may dispel the gloom of death; and after our departure hence in peace, and in thy favor, may we be received into thy everlasting kingdom, to enjoy, in union with the souls of our departed friends, the just reward of a pious and virtuous life. Amen."

A procession is then formed, which moves to the house of the deceased, and thence to the place of interment.

ORDER OF PROCESSION.

Tiler, with drawn sword.

Stewards, with white rods.

Musicians (if they are Masons), otherwise they follow the Tiler.

Master Masons.

Senior and Junior Deacons, with black rods.

Treasurer and Secretary.

Senior and Junior Wardens.

Past Masters.

The Holy Writings, on a cushion covered with black cloth, carried by a venerable brother.

THE MASTER.

The procession then moves to the house of the deceased, where it receives the

Clergy.

THE BODY,

with an apron lying on the coffin.

Pall Bearers.   Pall Bearers.

Mourners.

When the procession arrives at the place of interment, the brethren open ranks, and the procession moves in reverse order, the body being borne after the Master to the grave.

```
           PAST MASTERS.
        TREAS.              SEC'Y.
             CHAPLAIN.
  S. W.          •             J. W.
             W. M.
                •

  SEN. DEACON.                      JUN. DEACON.

  MASTER MASONS.     MARSHAL   PALL BEARERS   GRAVE   PALL BEARERS     MASTER MASONS.

             HOLY WRITINGS.


             •  •  •  •  •  •  •  •
  STEWARD.   •  •  MOURNERS.  •  •   STEWARD.
             •  •  •  •  •  •  •  •


                TILER.
                  •
```

The brethren then form around the grave, the officers of the Lodge and the clergy at the head, and the mourners at the foot. The service is resumed, and the following exhortation is given:

" Here we view a striking instance of the uncertainty of human life, and the vanity of human pursuits. The last offices paid to the dead are only useful as lectures to the living :—from them we are to derive instruction, and to consider every solemnity of this kind as a summons to prepare for our approaching dissolution.

" Notwithstanding the various mementoes of mortality, with which we daily meet; notwithstanding Death has established his empire over all the works of nature ; yet, through some unaccountable infatuation, we forget that we are born to die; we go on from one design to another, add hope to hope, and lay out plans for the employment of many years, till we are suddenly alarmed with the approach of Death, when we least expect him, and at an hour which we probably, conclude to be the meridian of our existence.

" What are all the externals of majesty, the pride of wealth, or the charms of beauty, when Nature has paid her just debt ? Fix your eyes on the last scene, and view life stript of her ornaments, and exposed in her natural meanness ; you will then be convinced of the futility of those empty delusions. In the grave, all fallacies are detected, all ranks are leveled, and all distinctions are done away.

" While we drop the sympathetic tear over the grave of our deceased friend, let charity incline

us to throw a veil over his foibles, whatever they
may have been, and not withhold from his memory the praise that his virtues may have claimed.
Suffer the apologies of human nature to plead in
his behalf. Perfection on earth has never been
attained :—the wisest, as well as the best of men,
have erred.

"Let the present example excite our most
serious thoughts, and strengthen our resolutions
of amendment. As life is uncertain, and all
earthly pursuits are vain, let us no longer post-
pone the all-important concern of preparing for
eternity ; but embrace the happy moment, while
time and opportunity offer, to provide against the
great change, when all the pleasures of this world
shall cease to delight, and the reflections of a
virtuous and holy life yield the only comfort and
consolation. Thus our expectations will not be
frustrated, nor we hurried unprepared into the
presence of an all-wise and powerful Judge, to
whom the secrets of all hearts are known.

"Let us, while in this state of existence, support with propriety the character of our profession, advert to the nature of our solemn ties, and
pursue with assiduity the sacred tenets of our
Order. Then, with becoming reverence, let us
seek the favor of the Eternal God, so that when
the awful moment of death arrives, be it soon or

late, we may be enabled to prosecute our journey, without dread or apprehension, to that far distant ' country, whence no traveler returns."

The following invocations are then made by the Master:

Master—" May we be true and faithful ; and may we live and die in love ! "

Response—" So mote it be."

Master—" May we profess what is good, and always act agreeably to our profession ! "

Response—" So mote it be."

Master—" May the Lord bless us and prosper us, and may all our good intentions be crowned with success ! "

Response—" So mote it be."

Master—" Glory to God in the highest ; on earth peace ! good-will towards men ! "

Response—" So mote it be, now, from henceforth, and forevermore.   Amen."

The apron is taken off the coffin and handed to the Master—the coffin is deposited in the grave—and the Master says :

" This Lamb Skin, or white leather Apron, is an emblem of Innocence, and the badge of a Mason ; more ancient than the Golden Fleece, or Roman Eagle ; more honorable than the Star and Garter, when worthily worn."

The Master then deposits it in the grave.

" This emblem I now deposit in the grave of
our deceased Brother. By this we are reminded
of the universal dominion of Death. The arm of
Friendship cannot oppose the King of Terrors,
nor the charms of innocence elude his grasp.
This grave, that coffin, this circle of mourning
friends, remind us that we, too, are mortal : soon
shall our bodies moulder to dust."

The Master holding the evergreen in his hand, continues :

" This *evergreen* is an emblem of our faith in
the immortality of the soul. By this we are reminded that we have an immortal part within us,
which shall survive the grave, and which shall
never, never, never die."

The brethren then move in procession around, 'and
severally drop * the sprig of evergreen into the grave ;
after which the *funeral grand honors* are given. The
Master then continues :

" From time immemorial, it has been the cus-
tom among the fraternity of Free and Accepted
Masons, at the request of a brother, to accompany
his remains to the place of interment, and there
to deposit them with the usual formalities.

* Advancing to the South side of the grave, hold out the right arm
horizontally and drop the sprig of evergreen on the breast of the coffin ;
then point the hand and look upward ; next bring the hand to the
left breast ; and finally down by the side.

"In conformity to this usage, we have assembled in the character of Masons, to offer up to his memory, before the world, the last tribute of our affection; thereby demonstrating the sincerity of our past esteem for him, and our steady attachment to the principles of the Order.

"The great Creator having been pleased, out of his infinite mercy, to remove our brother from the cares and troubles of a transitory existence, to a state of eternal duration, and thereby to weaken the chain by which we are united man to man, may we who survive him, anticipate our approaching fate, and be more strongly cemented in the ties of union and friendship; that, during the short space allotted to our present existence, we may wisely and usefully employ our time; and, in the reciprocal intercourse of kind and friendly acts, mutually promote the welfare and happiness of each other.

"Unto the grave we have resigned the body of our deceased brother; *earth to earth, dust to dust, ashes to ashes*, there to remain until the trump shall sound on the resurrection morn. We can cheerfully leave him in the hands of a Being who has done all things well; who is glorious in holiness, fearful in praises, doing wonders. Then let us all so improve this solemn warning, that on the great day of account we may receive from the compassionate Judge, the welcome invitation, 'Come, ye blessed of my Father, inherit the kingdom prepared for you from the foundation of the world.'"

"So mote it be. Amen."

"Almighty and eternal God, in whom we live, and move, and have our being—and before whom all men must appear in the judgment day to give an account of their deeds in life ; we, who are daily exposed to flying shafts of death, and now surround the grave of our fallen brother, most earnestly beseech thee to impress deeply on our minds the solemnities of this day, as well as the lamentable occurrence that has occasioned them. Here may we be forcibly reminded, that in the midst of life we are in death, and that whatever *elevation* of character we may have attained ; however *upright* and *square* the course we have pursued ; yet shortly must we all submit as victims of its destroying power, and endure the humbling *level* of the tomb, until the last loud trump shall sound the summons of our *resurrection* from mortality and *corruption.*

"May we have thy divine assistance, O merciful God, to redeem our misspent time ; and in the discharge of the important duties thou hast assigned us in the erection of our moral edifice, may we have *wisdom* from on high to direct us, *strength* commensurate with our *task* to support us, and the *beauty* of holiness to adorn and render all our performances acceptable in thy sight; and when our work is done, and our bodies mingle with the *mother earth*, may our souls, disengaged from their cumbrous dust, flourish and bloom in eternal day : and enjoy that rest which thou hast prepared for all good and faithful servants, in that spiritual house, not made with hands, eternal in the heavens. Amen."

" So mote it be. Amen."

The procession then returns in form to the place whence it set out, where the necessary duties are complied with, and the Lodge is closed in the Third degree.

A SHORTER FORM OF
BURIAL SERVICE,
TO BE USED AT THE GRAVE DURING VERY INCLEMENT WEATHER.

After the officers and brethren have taken their proper positions at the grave, the service begins by the following exhortation :

" BRETHREN :—We have assembled to-day as Masons, to offer to the memory of our deceased brother this last tribute of our affection. Unto the grave we now consign his body—earth to earth, ashes to ashes, dust to dust—there to remain until the trump shall sound on the Resurrection morn. We can trustfully leave him in the hands of Him who doeth all things well, who is 'glorious in holiness, fearful in praises, doing wonders.'"

The Master, then presenting the apron, continues :

" The lambskin apron is an emblem of innocence and the badge of a Mason."

The Master then deposits it in the grave.

"This emblem I now deposit in the grave of our deceased brother. We are here reminded of the universal dominion of Death."

The Master, holding the evergreen, continues :

" This evergreen is an emblem of our faith in the immortality of the soul. By it we are reminded that we have an immortal part within us which shall never, never, never die."

The brethren then move in procession around the place of interment and drop the sprig of evergreen into the grave. The funeral grand honors are then given, and the Master continues :

" To those of the immediate relatives and friends who are most heart-stricken at the loss they have sustained, we have but little of this world's consolation to offer. We can only sincerely, deeply, and most affectionately sympathize with them in their afflictive bereavement, and remind them that He who 'tempers the wind to the shorn lamb' looks down with infinite compassion upon the bereaved in the hour of their desolation, and will fold the arms of His love and protection around those who put their trust in Him."

"Almighty God, who hast taught us in thy holy word that thou dost not willingly afflict or grieve the children of men, have compassion upon thy servants here assembled. Remember us, O Lord, in mercy; endue our souls with patience under our affliction, and with resignation to thy blessed will. Lift up thy countenance upon us and give us peace, and pardon and save us for thy name's sake. Amen."

"So mote it be. Amen."

This concludes the service at the grave.

FORMS OF PETITIONS.

PETITION FOR DEGREES.

A petition for the degrees of Masonry shall be in writ
ing, signed by the applicant, and in the following form :

To the Master, Wardens, and Members of —— *Lodge,
No.* —, *A. F. & A. M.:*

The petition of ——, respectfully showeth that
he entertains a favorable opinion of your ancient
institution, and desires to be made a member
thereof. If this, his petition be granted, he will
yield a cheerful obedience to the customs and
usages of Masonry. His age is — years, his vocation that of a ——, and his residence ———.

Signed, ——— ———.

Date ———.

Recommended by

——— ———

——— ———

(84)

PETITION FOR MEMBERSHIP.

A petition for membership shall be in writing, signed by the applicant, in the following form, and shall be accompanied by the applicant's dimit:

To the Master, Wardens, and Members of —— Lodge, No. —, A. F. & A. M.:

The petition of ——, respectfully showeth that he was lately a member of —— Lodge, No. —, at ——, and he now prays to be admitted a member of your Lodge.   His age is — years, his vocation that of a ——, and his residence ———.

Signed,   ——— ———

Date ———.

Recommended by

——— ———

——— ———

———

CERTIFICATE FOR WIDOW OR ORPHANS OF A DECEASED MASON.

To all to whom these presents may come—Greeting:

Know Ye, That ——, whose name is written in the margin, is the —— of our late beloved brother, —— who *Departed this Life*, —— and who was at the time of his death, a member, in full and regular standing, of —— Lodge, No. —, of Ancient Free and Accepted Masons; which said Lodge was, at the time of his death, and still is, working under a Charter from the Grand Lodge of North Carolina. We would, therefore, most affectionately commend —— to the kindest offices of the Masonic Brotherhood everywhere.

Issued the —— day of ——, A. D. 18—, A. L. 58—.

———— ————, *W. M.*

Attest : ———— ————, *Secretary.*

ORDER OF BUSINESS.

(Uniform Code of By-Laws, Article IV., Sec. 3.)

The order of business at a regular communication shall be :

1. Reading minutes of last regular and all intervening communications.
2. Unfinished business.
3. Reports of committees on petitions for initiation and membership.
4. Balloting.
5. Reports of standing committees.
6. Reports of special committees.
7. Reception of petitions.
8. Communications.
9. Motions and resolutions.
10. Informal communications affecting the Craft.
11. Report of Orphan Asylum Committee.
12. Reading and approval of the minutes.